Road Trip

Activity Book for Kids

This book belongs to:

_____

_____

Our destination:

_____

Travel dates:

_____

~~from the author~~
from one parent to another

Welcome to "Road Trip Adventures," the ultimate activity book designed to make your journey as fun and entertaining as your destination!

As a mom of three adventurous kids who love to travel, I understand the challenges of keeping little ones engaged during long car rides, plane trips, and train journeys. That's why I created this activity book filled with exciting games, puzzles, and activities that have been tried and tested by my own children.
I have included some life hacks at the end that I hope will be useful to you. ♡

With "Road Trip Adventures" in hand, your kids are sure to have an unforgettable journey filled with laughter, learning, and lots of fun. So buckle up, hit the road, and get ready for the adventure of a lifetime!

Here you will find mix of the :

On-the-Go Games
In this section, your kids will find a variety of games perfect for playing while on the move. From classic car games like "I Spy" and "20 Questions" to creative storytelling prompts, these activities will keep boredom at bay and encourage imagination.

Travel Trivia
Challenge your kids' knowledge with fun and fascinating trivia questions about different destinations, landmarks, and modes of transportation. They'll learn interesting facts while having a blast competing to see who can answer the most questions correctly.

Creative Coloring
Let your children unleash their creativity with a collection of coloring pages featuring scenes from around the world. Whether they're coloring a bustling cityscape, a serene beach, or a majestic mountain range, these pages will inspire their imagination and artistic talents.

Puzzles
From word searches and mazes to crossword puzzles and cryptogram, this section is packed with brain-teasing challenges for kids of all ages. They'll have a blast solving puzzles while sharpening their problem-solving skills and boosting their confidence.

~ Daisy Stevens

Dot to dot

Connect the dots to see the whole picture

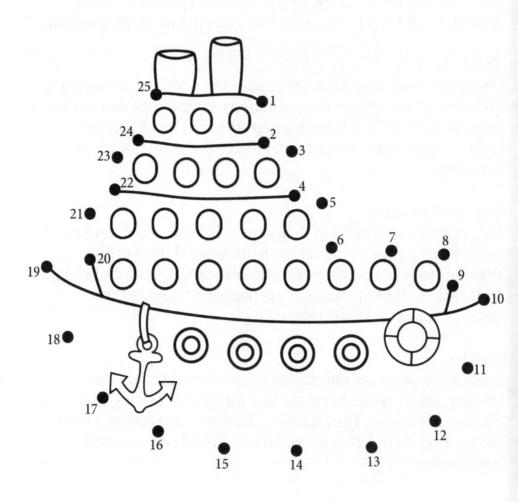

Coloring Time

Story Time

Start a story about traveling and take turns adding to it. Each person adds a sentence or two to continue the story.

Omg, Sam get lost his Flip Flops! Can you help him?

Crossword

Let's guess places of rest

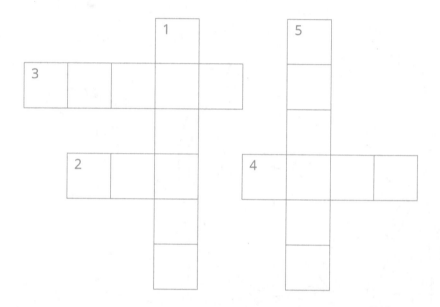

Across

3. A building where people stay when they are on vacation

2. A place where you can see lots of different animals, like lions, monkeys, and elephants

4. A natural area with tents, campfires, and hiking trails

Down

1. A place with palm trees and sandy beaches

5. A place where people go to see animals in their environment and learn about nature

Word Scramble

arC = _____

nTair = _____

enlaP = _____

Trpi = _____

aPck = _____

Maze

Can you help the girl
take the backpack?

Do you know?...

The Dead Sea, located between Israel
and Jordan, is so salty that you can
float effortlessly on its surface.

Try new game!

Counting Cars

Choose a color and count how many cars of that color pass by within a set time limit (e.g., five minutes).

Missing Vowels

ST _ T _ _

BR _ DG _

P _ L _ C _

P _ R _ M _ D

_ RCH

L _ GHTH _ _ S _

Do you know?...

The Sahara Desert in Africa is the largest hot desert in the world, covering an area almost as big as the United States!

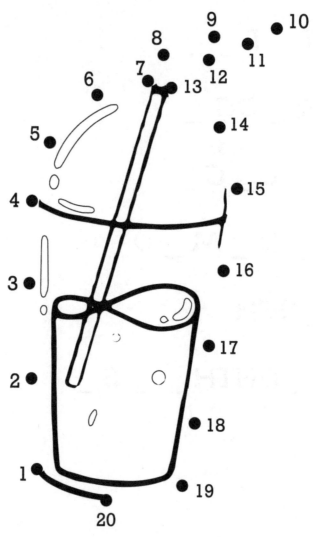

Cryptogram

Assign a different symbol or letter to represent each letter of the alphabet. Using your code key, replace each letter in your secret message with its corresponding symbol or letter.
Write down the encoded message.

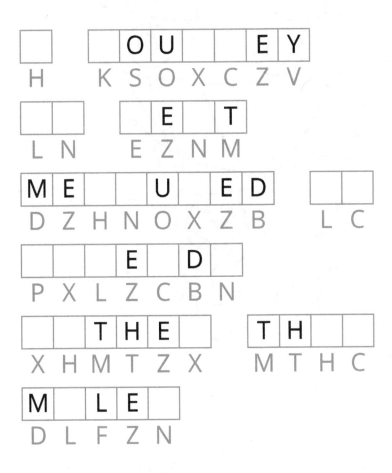

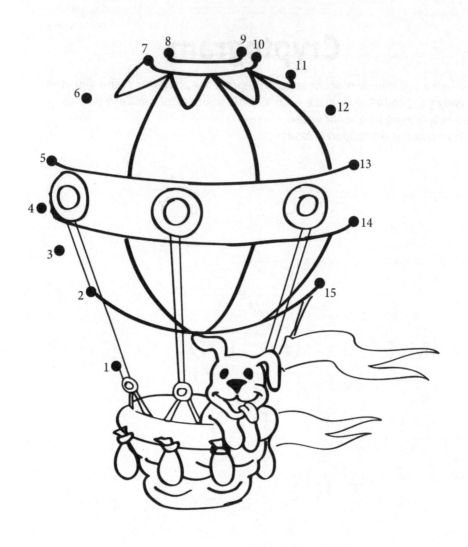

Do you know?...

The Great Barrier Reef in Australia is so big that it can be seen from outer space.

Maze

Help the bus get passengers to the beach

Word Scramble

cnoaVtai   = _____

nerAuvdet   = _____

edGiu   = _____

frcfTia   = _____

prDuateer   = _____

Do you know?...

There's a pink lake in Australia called Lake Hillier where the water is naturally pink.

Try new game!

I'm Spy!

One player chooses an object within sight and says, "I spy with my little eye, something that is [color]." Other players take turns guessing what the object is.

Word Scramble

ruTo   = _____

Ttkcie   = _____

ieDrv   = _____

iittnoanesD   = _____

prrotAi   = _____

Word Search

Please find all the words listed below

M	T	S	K	Q	A	U	V	X	C	V	N	B	O
D	Z	F	T	D	I	N	O	S	A	U	R	K	E
Z	U	X	A	G	C	C	L	C	V	M	C	K	L
T	V	N	D	O	C	Y	E	E	E	N	F	W	E
I	W	A	V	W	P	M	C	A	S	T	L	E	P
T	O	O	E	K	Z	B	E	V	T	F	T	K	H
W	X	J	N	E	I	W	A	E	K	B	K	H	A
Q	P	T	T	R	G	K	W	Q	C	E	Z	A	N
O	D	R	U	Q	Q	I	U	B	E	A	K	P	T
G	G	N	R	K	M	U	M	O	H	C	Y	S	N
H	O	D	E	Y	I	W	Y	C	R	H	C	C	F
C	X	B	K	H	E	X	Y	V	B	M	O	F	T
T	E	F	T	K	E	D	C	Y	X	S	R	O	H
X	D	O	S	D	Y	X	F	B	P	M	W	U	Y

Beach
Elephant
Dinosaur

Castle
Adventure

Mine Finder

There are several mines hidden randomly within a grid.
Your task is to determine the location of these mines and mark them. To assist
you in figuring out the location of the mines, some squares in the grid have a
number in them. This number indicates the number of mines that are hidden in
adjacent squares to that particular square, both diagonally and orthogonally.
Squares that include a number cannot contain a mine. Meanwhile, white squares
may contain a mine or may be empty.

				1				
			3	1				
1	2		2	1				
	1	1	1					
					1	1	1	
				1	2		1	
				1			2	1
				1	1	2		
						1		

Missing Vowels

B _ _ CH

_ SL _ ND

F _ R _ ST

C _ N _ _ N

GL _ C _ _ R

S _ F _ R _

Do you know?...

The Great Wall of China is so long that it could wrap around the Earth more than twice!

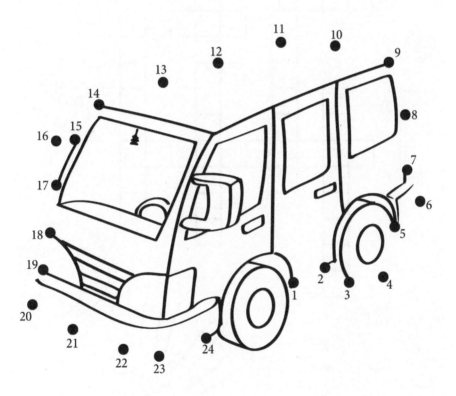

Crossword

Find all objects

Do you know?...

Australia is home to the world's largest living
structure, the Great Barrier Reef, which is made
up of thousands of individual reefs and islands.

Try new game!

Alphabet Game

Find objects outside or inside the vehicle that start with each letter of the alphabet, in order.

Do you know?...

The Great Barrier Reef in
Australia is so big that it can be
seen from outer space.

Cryptogram

	E		O	L	
H	P	Z	O	D	K	X	S

	S		A		B	O	O	K
E	I	V	W	D	D	U

A			T	O	S	E
V	J	S	H	P	D	I	Z

		O			O			O	T
O	P	D	S	D	J	D	H

T	A	E	L			E	A	
H	K	V	Q	Z	X	K	Z	V	S

O	L			O		E
D	J	X	M	D	J	Z

P	A	G	E
F	V	A	Z

Do you know?...

Mount Everest, the tallest mountain on Earth, is still growing by about a quarter of an inch every year!

Word Search

J J I N Z P V O G W F W P R K
V Z N L M R H M E R M A I D C
Y Z K I T T X U U X R Q R E P
J E M G I Q L G V L D S A O S
O D I H B Q D D D C E A T U Y
F M A T U P L A I C O C E A N
V H F H Q O D S U V K Q P M A
H C D O J F F C K Q V T T B A
C W R U E J J I M C J L V Z R
N V W S B F V I O Q M Q A P Q
G W S E F G I X I K O N Z D P
V J J I I G A M H I L T X K X
Y Q U E E N P R U J W N E D H
L H N R A K O P W U C L J E J
O L O Z W Y L Q T R I O O R L

Ocean

Mermaid

Pirate

Queen

Lighthouse

Dot to dot

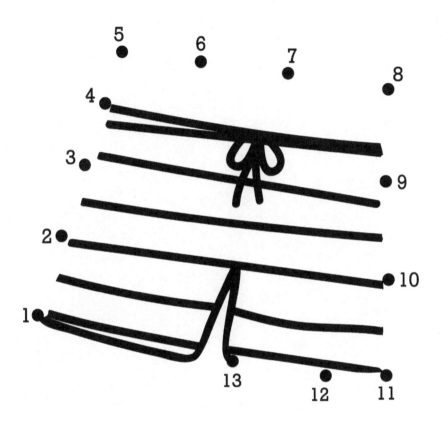

Do you know?...

There's a country called Liechtenstein in Europe that is so small you could walk across it in just a few hours!

Crossword

Across
2. A place where you can see colorful fish, sharks, and other marine animals.
3. A place with lots of flowers, trees, and sometimes even butterflies.
4. A big, old building where kings and queens used to live.

Down
1. A place where you can see paintings, sculptures, and artifacts
5. A tall tower with a bright light at the top to guide ships at sea.

Do you know?...

Japan has more than 1,500 earthquakes every year because it sits on the "Ring of Fire," a zone with lots of volcanic activity.

Try new game!

Counting Cars

Choose a color and count how many cars of that color pass by within a set time limit (e.g., five minutes).

Missing Vowels

SHR _ N _

M _ S _ _ M

Z _ _

C _ TH _ DR _ L

M _ RK _ T

G _ RD _ N

Do you know?...

Norway is home to thousands of fjords, which are long, narrow inlets with steep sides, carved by glaciers.

Word Search

U O W K J X D K K R W X F V
I S R I A G X J T I J J O Q
Q H P Q U E Q U S J Y P P O
R V E F Z M X N L I A E T H
D I I F D Z E B R A C R L U
N W O I K Q G R X Q H P U K
O S I T W H P J Y X T W X S
F W A T E R F A L L Z L R K
J S O N I H N E O V S N C J
K F S M C Y T N P F L V N Y
A H I B G I W M H F P R W R
B I C A K T O G O M B O O B
G C R N P Y M Y N U J Q M B
X I G W G A L I E N Q K B I

Yacht

Waterfall

Alien

Zebra

Xylophone

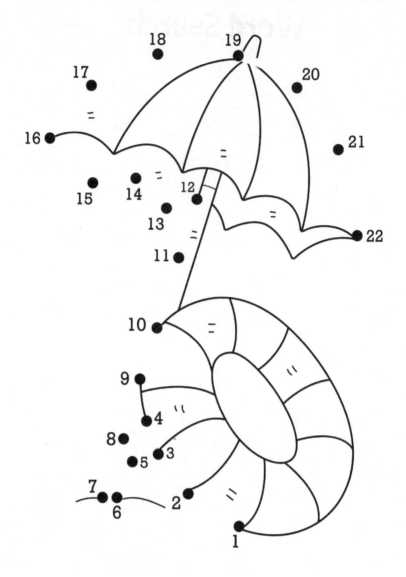

Do you know?...

The city of Venice, Italy, is built on more than 100 small islands connected by canals and bridges.

Word Scramble

Heolt = _____

Rtenal = _____

layDe = _____

kHei = _____

gsSghiinete = _____

Do you know?...

The Angkor Wat temple complex in Cambodia is the largest religious monument in the world, covering an area of over 400 acres.

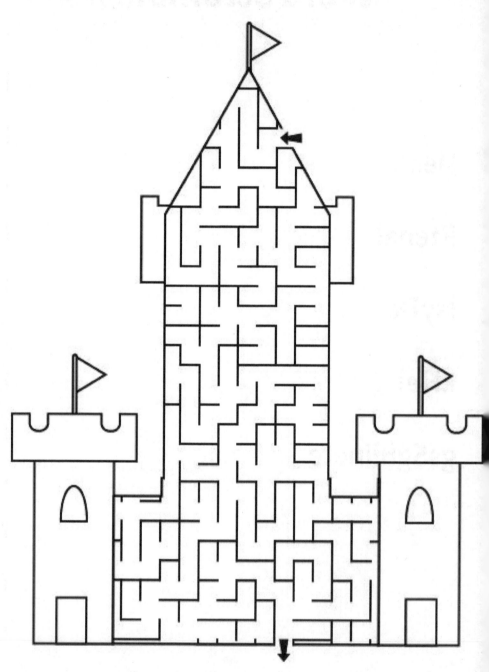

Cryptogram

Dot to dot

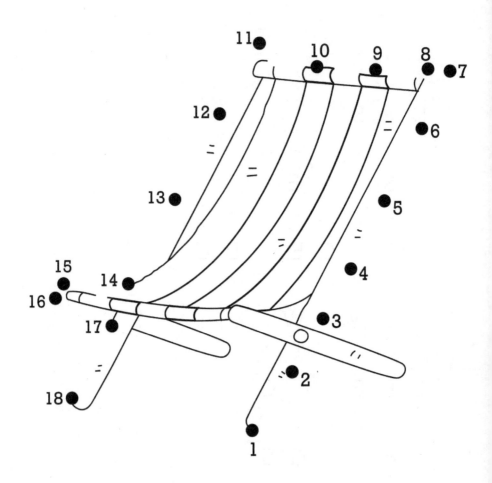

Do you know?...

The island of Maui in Hawaii is home to a dormant volcano called Haleakalā, which means "House of the Sun" in Hawaiian. Visitors can watch breathtaking sunrises from its summit.

Mine Finder

	1			1		1									
1	1			1		2	1	1							
				2				1						1	1
				1				2	2	2	3	2	1	2	
				1	1	2									
	1	1	1			1									
1	2		1	1	1	2	2	3							
						2		1	1	2	1	1	1	1	1
						3									
						2					1	1	2	1	
						1				1	1	2			
						2	2	2	1	1			3	1	
								1	1	2			1		
					2	2	2	2	1		2		1		
					1				1	2	2	3		1	1
					1				1						

Missing Vowels

T _ W _ R

C _ STL _

T _ MPL _

R _ _ NS

F _ _ NT _ _ N

M _ _ NT _ _ N

Do you know?...

The island of Santorini in Greece is famous for its stunning sunsets, which are considered some of the most beautiful in the world.

Dot to dot

Join the dots to see the whole picture

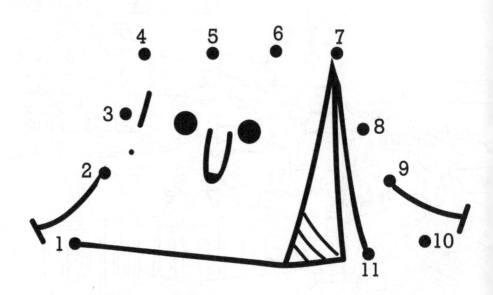

Do you know?...

The Amazon Rainforest produces about 20% of the world's oxygen, making it incredibly important for our planet.

Word Search

```
Q L V A J S P D G A R D E N P Q L K
F E B U V X T T C V I C Z L I F G G
V O N N A S P Z O R N R U U T G F V
W O J W Y O S J C J K T L Y T L V M
K N E U T S X A D C A L A I Q I V P
U S Q I M F T U L Y L O H V O V U G
G U S C Q K I T E Y S N A Q V N C O
D K R I C F Z J M O V H N P E G N M
Y S I H D E T S O P J I S L A N D Q
D Z S G U R Q K N K H V K N T F J G
A H O T A I R B A L L O O N B G Y S
K Q R C B U K O D G R M D U O V R G
R W G L S I X E E C C H F K N H P Q
D F X D L E K S H V O C M Y J P A P
U N K H Y F G Y Q X M V S Z Y Z L J
Y N Z X U D B Y V K Z W F F W Q Z B
U Q Y H Z O B X E U D U R H Q A Z Z
U U Z Y Y M J F H M B J H F S B V T
```

Kite
Lemonade
Island

Garden
Hot Air Balloon

Find a way out of the maze

Do you know?...

The Eiffel Tower in Paris grows taller in the summer due to the expansion of iron when it gets hot.

Try new game!

Animal Spotting

Look out for animals along the journey and keep track of how many different ones you see.

Word Scramble

sBu   = _____

pShi   = _____

Roda   = _____

paM   = _____

klaW   = _____

Dot to dot

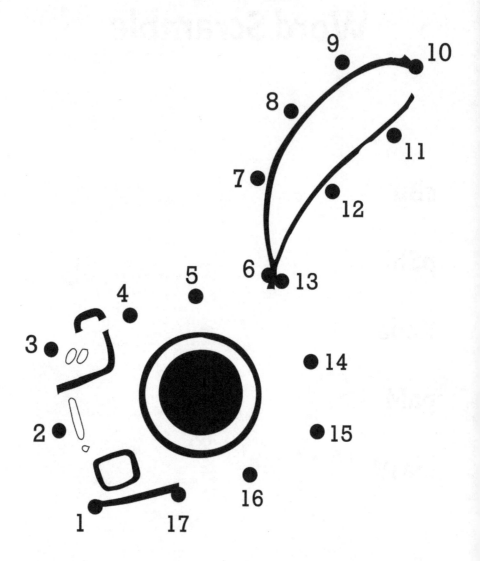

Do you know?...

The Nile River in Egypt is the longest river in the world, stretching over 4,000 miles!

Cryptogram

			T	R		E	
Z	K		Z	Y	B	L	P	S

I	S		T	
E	F		Z	K

D	I	S	C			E	R
G	E	F	W	K	L	P	Y

T			T	
Z	U	B	Z

E		E	R	Y			E		I	S
P	L	P	Y	R	K	O	P		E	F

W	R			
I	Y	K	O	V

	B			T
B	A	K	T	Z

	T		E	R
K	Z	U	P	Y

C			T	R	I	E	S
W	K	T	O	Z	Y	E	P	F

Crossword

Word Search

```
B  Z  A  S  F  X  P  B  W  H  L  S  Z  M  S
H  G  F  V  V  A  M  P  I  R  E  A  B  K  X
J  R  N  G  N  F  V  C  Z  T  Z  I  Z  Z  H
U  E  D  M  H  Y  O  T  A  U  N  S  I  G  J
P  A  P  N  M  P  N  H  R  I  I  P  G  J  Z
Q  X  H  H  C  R  W  T  D  P  L  A  K  T  I
U  G  K  B  S  T  T  L  D  P  O  C  V  X  W
J  N  R  U  N  D  E  R  W  A  T  E  R  D  Z
I  O  M  D  K  R  T  X  B  U  C  S  M  V  T
Y  Y  I  O  S  S  N  H  N  T  N  H  X  M  P
V  D  X  K  J  C  F  F  B  L  Z  I  L  G  A
D  J  Y  Q  T  E  L  E  S  C  O  P  E  L  D
I  X  X  Q  N  T  H  N  O  F  W  L  M  X  H
Y  B  U  L  G  Q  K  K  P  F  D  V  F  B  J
L  G  L  Z  V  K  E  F  U  F  T  X  A  A  C
```

Wizard
Telescope
Spaceship

Vampire
Underwater

Dot to dot

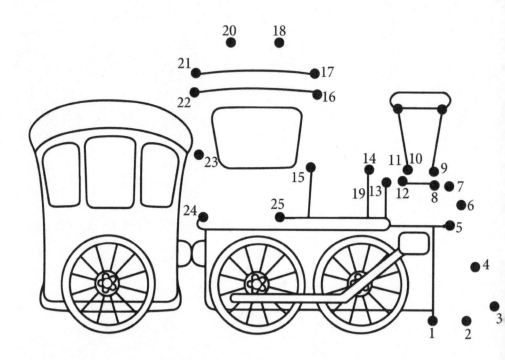

Do you know?...

Maglev trains use magnetic levitation to glide above the tracks, eliminating friction and allowing for incredibly fast speeds. The fastest commercially operating maglev train, the Shanghai Maglev, reaches speeds of up to 268 mph (431 km/h).

Try new game!

Word Association

Someone says a word (e.g., "dog"), and the next person has to say a word that's related to it (e.g., "cat"). Keep going with the association chain as long as you can.

Missing Vowels

W _ T _ RF _ LL

C _ V _

D _ S _ RT

V _ LC _ N _

R _ _ F

_ _ S _ S

Find a way out of the maze

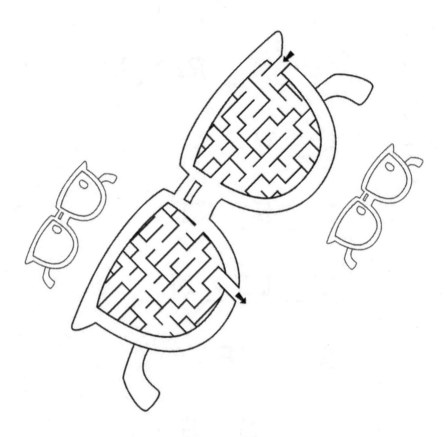

Do you know?...

The African savanna is home to some of the fastest land animals on Earth, including cheetahs, which can reach speeds of up to 70 miles per hour in short bursts.

Crossword

4			2	
5				
	1			
3				

Across

1. This has wheels and takes you from one place to another on the road
3. This flies high in the sky and takes people to faraway places
4. What do you use to float on water, go fishing, or explore rivers and lakes?

Down

2. This travels on tracks and carries passengers across long distances
5. This carries many people and travels on roads, usually with scheduled stops

Word Scramble

Txai = _____

agggueL = _____

yJonreu = _____

tprsPaos = _____

Retuo = _____

Dot to dot

Do you know?...

The first successful powered airplane flight was achieved by the Wright brothers, Orville and Wilbur, on December 17, 1903, near Kitty Hawk, North Carolina, USA. Their plane, the Wright Flyer, flew for 12 seconds, covering a distance of 120 feet.

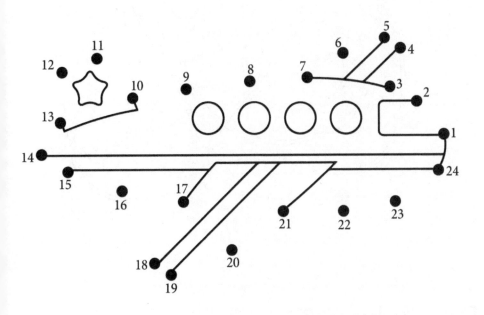

Choose the way

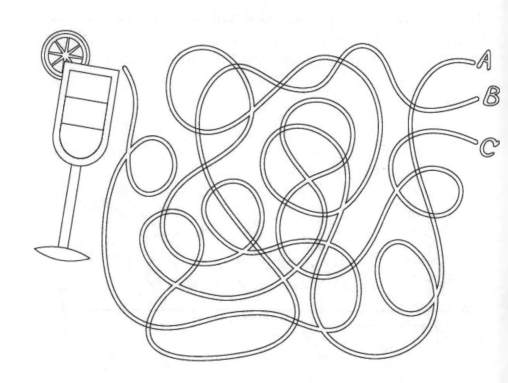

Do you know?...

The island nation of Japan has over
6,800 islands, but only around 430
of them are inhabited.

Do you know?...

The Colosseum in Rome, Italy, used to be filled with water to host mock sea battles!

Try new game!

Guess the Song

Hum or whistle a tune, and the others have to guess the song. You can take turns being the one who hums or whistles.

Missing Vowels

_ BS _ RV _ T _ R _

_ Q _ _ R _ _ M

P _ RK

M _ SQ _ _

SQ _ _ R _

ST _ D _ _ M

Cryptogram

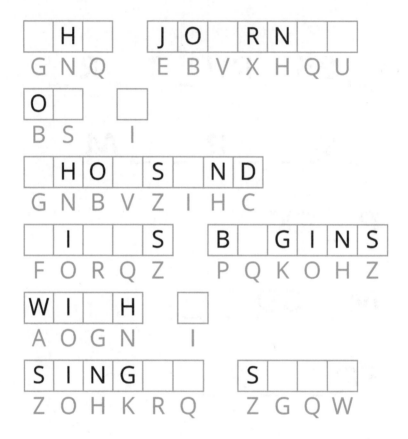

Dot to dot

Do you know?...

There's a natural phenomenon in the Maldives called bioluminescent plankton, where the water glows blue at night when disturbed, creating a magical effect.

Find a way out of the maze to take perfect photo

Choose the way

Do you know?...

In Iceland, you can find geysers that shoot hot water high into the air, sometimes reaching heights of over 100 feet!

Missing Vowels

TH _ _ TR _

L _ NDM _ RK

M _ N _ M _ NT

STR _ _ T

Do you know?...

The Galápagos Islands in Ecuador are famous for their unique animals, including giant tortoises and blue-footed boobies.

Try new game!

20 Questions

One player thinks of an object, and the others take turns asking up to 20 yes-or-no questions to guess what it is. Whoever guesses correctly gets to think of the next object.

Dot to dot

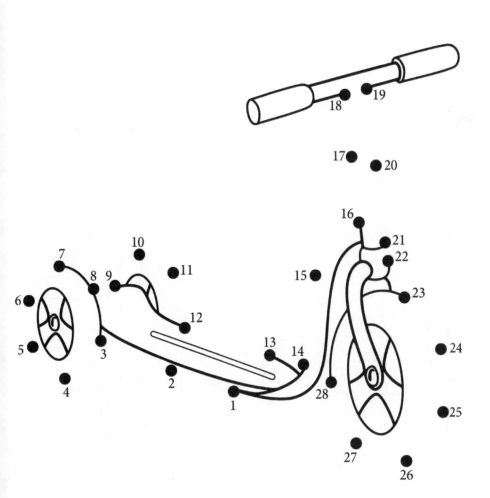

Do you know?...

The smallest country in the world is Vatican City,
which is entirely surrounded by the city of Rome,
Italy. It's also the headquarters of the Roman
Catholic Church.

Find a way out of the maze

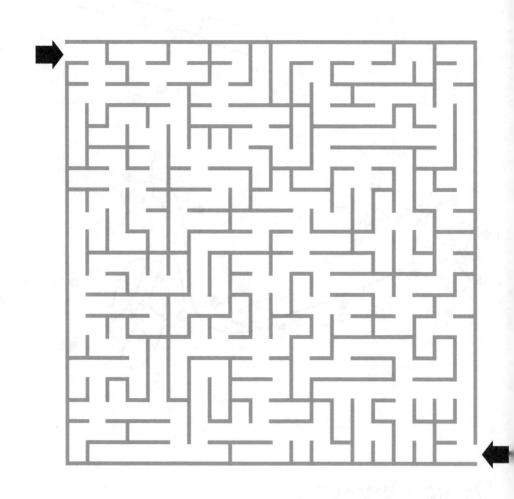

Mine Finder

1	1	1					1	1
		2	1	1			1	
1	2			1			1	
	1		2	1		1	1	
	2		2		1	2		
	1		1		1			
1	2	1	1		2			
	1				1			

Word Scramble

ieacsSut   = _____

arcTiff   = _____

tuhSelt   = _____

Cpma   = _____

avgointiNa   = _____

Dot to dot

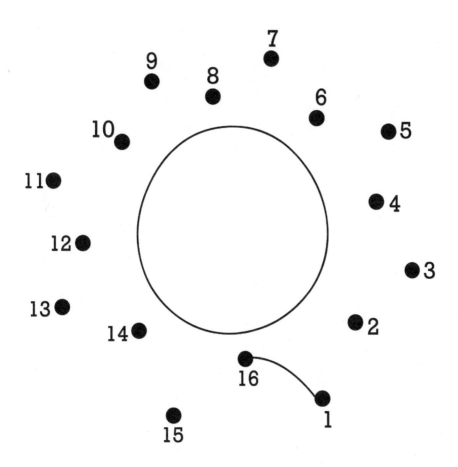

Do you know?...

The city of Istanbul in Turkey is located on two continents—Europe and Asia—making it the only city in the world to straddle two continents.

Word Search

```
E  J  E  V  C  M  B  F  R  T  G  V  X  S  K  D  J
N  S  M  O  N  I  K  S  N  C  E  Y  E  A  A  V  W
F  M  F  O  M  A  X  U  I  G  U  Z  N  G  U  M  Q
S  C  Q  V  Z  M  L  O  S  A  N  G  E  L  E  S  S
P  J  J  B  A  I  D  E  Y  P  W  P  W  H  I  Y  A
U  V  W  U  A  B  F  F  F  S  D  R  Y  E  K  O  N
S  I  E  C  D  W  C  H  I  C  A  G  O  M  M  P  F
A  G  S  F  M  Y  Y  W  N  L  M  Z  R  B  R  I  R
K  W  X  W  S  S  B  R  W  I  R  K  K  D  J  C  A
T  A  L  U  C  Q  E  X  V  O  A  P  W  O  A  A  N
M  L  N  O  B  B  R  R  B  F  I  C  Q  B  W  L  C
A  V  F  L  A  M  J  U  H  I  P  B  X  X  M  U  I
D  D  G  M  D  F  V  M  J  L  S  E  B  O  I  M  S
Q  I  E  F  M  O  F  H  E  V  W  N  A  D  C  S  C
Z  T  K  P  B  I  C  L  D  X  Q  E  K  T  F  M  O
E  Y  B  O  O  J  Z  E  D  L  X  P  K  N  F  Y  T
Q  H  S  X  Z  V  A  O  U  F  Z  T  E  I  Q  B  K
```

Miami   Chicago   New York
Los Angeles   San Francisco

Dot to dot

Do you know?...

The invention of the steam engine revolutionized transportation in the 19th century. The first commercially successful steam-powered locomotive, built by George Stephenson, was called the "Rocket" and began operating in 1829 in England.

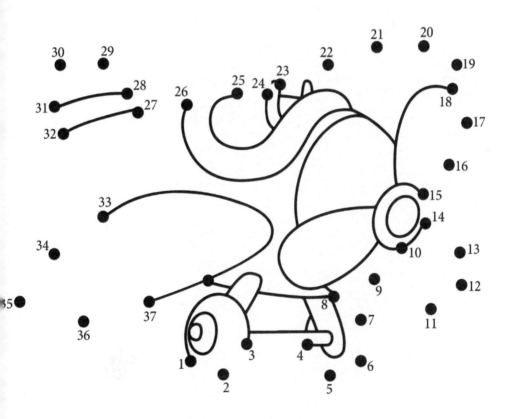

Find a way out of the maze

Do you know?...

The name "Golden Gate" actually refers to the entrance to the San Francisco Bay from the Pacific Ocean, which was named by early explorers in reference to the Golden Horn harbor in Istanbul, Turkey.

Try new game!

Category Game

Choose a category like animals, foods, or colors. Take turns naming items within that category without repeating. If someone can't think of an item or repeats one, they're out.

Find a way out of the maze

Crossword

Across
1. What country is famous for the Eiffel Tower and the Louvre Museum?
2. What country is known for its leaning tower in Pisa and delicious pasta?
3. What country is known for its sushi, cherry blossoms, and Mount Fuji?

Down
4. What country is known for its unique animals like kangaroos and koalas, as well as the Sydney Opera House and the Great Barrier Reef?
5. What country is famous for its maple syrup, Niagara Falls, and the Rocky Mountains?

Mine Finder

	1				1			
	1			1	1		1	1
1	1			1			1	
				1			1	1
				1				
				2	1	2	1	1
1	1	1						
		2		3	1	2	1	1
		1		1				

Dot to dot

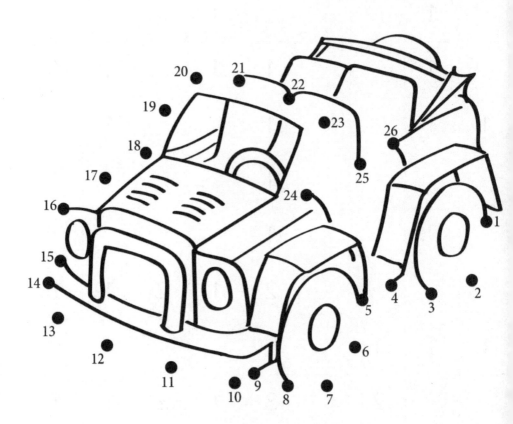

Do you know?...

The invention of the automobile is credited to Karl Benz, who built the first practical motor vehicle powered by an internal combustion engine in 1885. His creation, the Benz Patent-Motorwagen, is considered the world's first automobile.

Try new game!

Alphabet Memory Game

Start with the phrase "I'm going on a trip and I'm bringing..." followed by something that starts with the letter A. The next person repeats the phrase, adds their own item starting with B, and so on. Each player must remember all the previous items in alphabetical order.

Word Scramble

Eorxepl   = _____

urseCi   = _____

Bacpkakc   = _____

alrAriv   = _____

gniradBo   = _____

Word Search

```
J  M  J  U  X  T  F  Z  F  F  F  S  G  S  K
Z  N  V  S  I  R  M  A  S  V  G  D  D  S  U
N  E  S  B  Q  Y  W  L  G  Z  M  M  J  I  L
G  T  H  Y  R  O  A  A  M  A  X  R  I  Q  Z
D  V  B  Z  D  Y  S  B  R  T  I  P  M  J  I
U  O  D  X  J  C  H  Y  O  B  Y  U  N  H  V
L  P  I  A  J  Z  I  T  Z  R  N  B  Y  J  Z
A  M  Q  H  Q  J  N  Q  L  N  Z  Q  T  A  Q
S  Z  S  D  P  U  G  B  O  S  T  O  N  J  W
V  Z  U  T  O  Q  T  U  I  E  L  I  J  M  Y
E  Y  J  B  E  C  O  X  T  A  T  O  X  Y  C
G  T  J  A  A  D  N  K  O  T  X  J  W  M  T
A  I  T  M  W  D  M  R  U  T  Q  G  V  R  M
S  V  D  Z  N  E  W  O  R  L  E  A  N  S  X
D  O  H  J  M  U  A  A  X  E  P  C  W  F  V
```

Boston   Seattle   Las Vegas
Washington   New Orleans

Find a way out of the maze

Do you know?...

The Great Sphinx of Giza in Egypt has the body
of a lion and the head of a human, and it's one
of the largest and oldest statues in the world.

Crossword

Across
1. What do you use to keep warm and cook food when you're camping?
5. What's the name for the designated area where people set up their tents when camping?

Down
2. What do you sleep in when you go camping?
3. What do you use to see in the dark while camping?
4. What do you carry your clothes and supplies in when you go camping?

Dot to dot

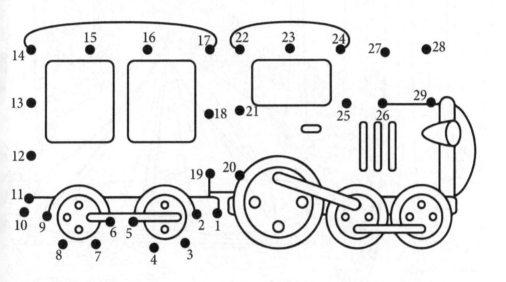

Do you know?...

The Orient Express was a famous luxury train service that operated between Paris and Istanbul from 1883 to 2009. It was renowned for its opulent accommodations and scenic routes through Europe and Asia.

Do you know?...

There's a village in India called Shani Shingnapur where no doors have locks, and no thefts have been reported for centuries!

Try new game!

Storytelling Relay

Start a story with a few sentences and then have each person add a sentence to continue the story. Go around in a circle, with each person adding a new sentence to keep the story going.

Word Search

Q Y B P L U J S O N Y P P C W F I

N X F K O M S J O O H H E Y N V U

V Q S J L W E P O G B I J X I C Z

K Q L X V I D O L Z E L E W F D Y

S Z G O F I F L K Q A A I Z H I K

U U Z R P J L G U N C D S Y D Q A

E G I L D P E D E N V E R U P L F

Z C P A I S N P M B C L F I P C H

T F K N J S D F A B T P A N Q U K

D H X D V Z A P T X A H U S Z Y M

L B U O P A M A Q N T I D X M Z A

T U D F E S G D U M L A U U I Y W

U Y P Q K L L T U R A C A G J M Z

R J A R P N R N S A N D I E G O K

L J R I G Y D R N V T X G X K S L

K T F Q P Y D F P C A L Z U T B J

X A J N G C M S Y T F G A O O Z V

Denver
San Diego
Atlanta

Orlando
Philadelphia

Find a way out of the maze

Dot to dot

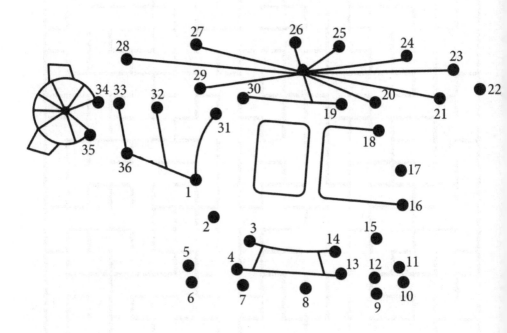

Do you know?...

New Zealand is home to the world's only flightless parrot, the kakapo, which is also one of the rarest birds in the world.

Find a way out of the maze

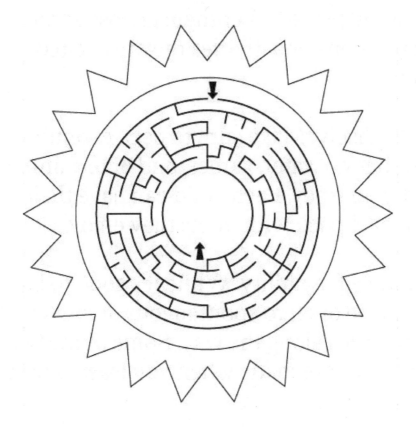

Do you know?...

The city of Rio de Janeiro in Brazil is famous for its annual Carnival celebration, which features colorful parades, samba music, and elaborate costumes.

Tips for Enjoying Your Family Road Trip Adventure:

Plan Together: Involve your children in the planning process. Let them choose some destinations or activities they're excited about.

Pack Wisely: Make sure to pack essentials like snacks, water, games, and entertainment for the journey. Each child can have their own backpack with items they enjoy.

Embrace Flexibility: While it's good to have a plan, be open to spontaneous detours and discoveries along the way. Some of the best memories are made when you least expect them!

Keep it Engaging: Plan activities to keep everyone entertained during the drive. Games like "I Spy," audiobooks, or a family playlist can make the journey more enjoyable.

Take Breaks: Regular breaks for stretching, snacks, and bathroom stops are essential, especially with kids. Look for interesting rest stops or parks where the children can burn off some energy.

Try Local Cuisine: Explore the local food scene at your destination. Let your children sample new dishes and flavors—it's a delicious way to experience different cultures.

Be Present: Put away distractions like phones and gadgets during family time. Enjoy the sights, sounds, and experiences together as a family.

Capture Memories: Encourage your kids to take photos or draw pictures of their favorite moments. A travel journal or diary can be a great way to document the trip together.

Thank You
for Embarking on This Adventure!

Dear Fellow Adventurers,

Thank you for choosing to journey with us through the pages of our road trip books! As a writer, a mom of three, and a passionate traveler, crafting these adventures for families like yours has been an absolute joy.

I believe that the best stories are those we create together, and I hope that our road trip books have sparked countless moments of laughter, learning, and discovery in your family. Your support means the world to me, and I'm deeply grateful for the opportunity to be a part of your travel adventures.

If you enjoyed the journey as much as we did, I would be incredibly grateful if you could take a moment to share your feedback on our Amazon page. Your thoughts and experiences not only help us improve but also inspire other families to embark on their own unforgettable adventures.

Thank you once again for choosing our road trip books. Here's to many more adventures together!

Warmest regards,

Daisy Stevens
Author, Mom, and Travel Enthusiast

Bonus materials

Embark on a Journey with Daisy's Travel Tales!

Are you ready to ignite your child's sense of wonder and curiosity? Join us on an adventure-filled voyage with our printable PDF diary for little travelers – absolutely FREE!

Inside, your child will discover:
- 🌍 Fun prompts to record their travel memories
- 🎨 Engaging activities to spark creativity
- 📝 Space to jot down fascinating facts and observations

Claim your FREE sample now and let the adventures begin! Simply enter your email on tripbook.my.canva.site/dairy to download your printable diary and start making memories that will last a lifetime.

Scan me!

Solutions Crossword

			1 R				5 S		
3 H	o	t	e	l			a		
			s				f		
	2 Z	o	o		4 C	a	m	p
			r				r		
			t				i		

Across
2. A place where you can see lots of different animals, like lions, monkeys, and elephants
3. A building where people stay when they are on vacation
4. A natural area with tents, campfires, and hiking trails

Down
1. A place with palm trees and sandy beaches
5. A place where people go to see animals in their environment and learn about nature

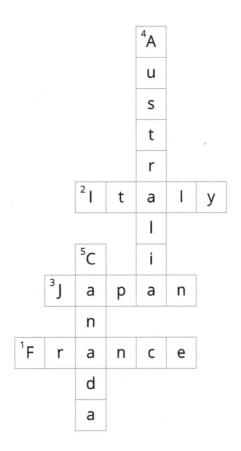

Across

1. What country is famous for the Eiffel Tower and the Louvre Museum?
2. What country is known for its leaning tower in Pisa and delicious pasta?
3. What country is known for its sushi, cherry blossoms, and Mount Fuji?

Down

4. What country is known for its unique animals like kangaroos and koalas, as well as the Sydney Opera House and the Great Barrier Reef?
5. What country is famous for its maple syrup, Niagara Falls, and the Rocky Mountains?

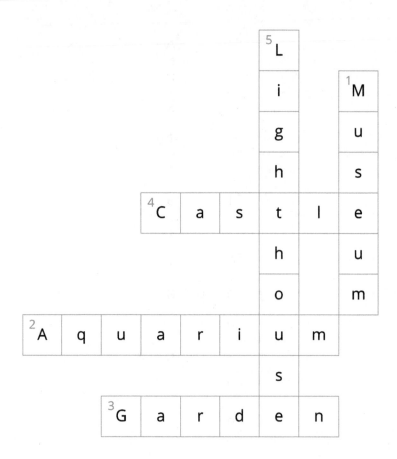

Across

2. A place where you can see colorful fish, sharks, and other marine animals.
3. A place with lots of flowers, trees, and sometimes even butterflies.
4. A big, old building where kings and queens used to live.

Down

1. A place where you can see paintings, sculptures, and artifacts
5. A tall tower with a bright light at the top to guide ships at sea.

Crossword Puzzle

4			2	
b	o	a	t	
5 u			r	
s		1 c	a	r
			i	
3 p	l	a	n	e

Across
1. This has wheels and takes you from one place to another on the road
3. This flies high in the sky and takes people to faraway places
4. What do you use to float on water, go fishing, or explore rivers and lakes?

Down
2. This travels on tracks and carries passengers across long distances
5. This carries many people and travels on roads, usually with scheduled stops

Minefinder solutions

2	💣	4	💣	💣	1			
2	💣	5	💣	3	1			
1	2	💣	2	1				
	1	1	1					
					1	1	1	
				1	2	💣	1	
				1	💣	3	2	1
				1	1	2	💣	2
						1	2	💣

1	1	1				1	1	
1	💣	2	1	1		1	💣	
1	2	3	💣	1		1	1	
	1	💣	2	1		1	1	1
	2	2	2		1	2	💣	1
	1	💣	1		1	💣	3	2
1	2	1	1		2	2	3	💣
💣	1				1	💣	2	1

	1	💣	2	💣	1			
	1	1	2	1	1		1	1
1	1	2	1	1			1	💣
1	💣	2	💣	1			1	1
2	2	2	1	1				
💣	1	1	1	2	1	2	1	1
1	1	1	💣	2	💣	2	💣	1
		2	2	3	1	2	1	1
		1	💣	1				

Missing Vowel solutions

Statue

Tower

Bridge

Castle

Palace

Temple

Pyramid

Ruins

Arch

Fountain

Lighthouse

Mountain

Beach

Waterfall

Island

Cave

Forest

Desert

Canyon

Volcano

Glacier

Reef

Safari

Oasis

Shrine

Observatory

Museum

Aquarium

Zoo

Park

Cathedral

Mosque

Market

Square

Garden

Stadium

Theatre

Monument

Landmark

Street

Word Scrumble solutions

Car	Vacation
Bus	Explore
Train	Adventure
Ship	Cruise
Plane	Guide
Road	Backpack
Trip	Traffic
Map	Arrival
Pack	Departure
Walk	Boarding
Tour	Hotel
Taxi	Suitcase
Ticket	Rental
Luggage	Traffic
Drive	Delay
Journey	Shuttle
Destination	Hike
Passport	Camp
Airport	Sightseeing
Route	Navigation

Word search solutions

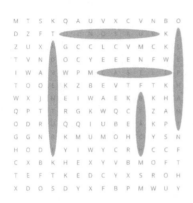

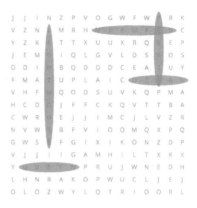

Beach   Castle   Dinosaur
Elephant   Adventure

Ocean   Queen   Pirate
Mermaid   Lighthouse

Yacht   Zebra   Alien
Waterfall   Xylophone

Kite   Garden   Island
Lemonade   Hot Air Balloon

B	Z	A	S	F	X	P	B	H	L	S	Z	M	S
H	G	F	V	A	M	P	I	R	A	B	K	X
J	R	N	G	N	F	V	C	T	Z	I	Z	Z	H
U	E	D	M	H	Y	O	T	A	U	N	I	G	J
P	A	P	N	M	P	N	H	I	I	G	J	Z
Q	X	H	H	C	R	W	T	P	L	A	K	T	I
U	G	K	B	S	T	T	L	D	P	O	C	V	X	W
J	N	R	U	N	D	E	R	W	A	T	D	Z
I	O	M	D	K	R	T	X	B	U	C	S	M	V	T
Y	Y	I	O	S	S	N	H	N	T	N	X	M	P
V	D	X	K	J	C	F	F	B	L	Z	L	G	A
D	J	Y	Q	S	E	L	E	S	C	O	L	D
I	X	X	Q	N	T	H	N	O	F	W	L	M	X	H
Y	B	U	L	G	Q	K	K	P	F	D	V	F	B	J
L	G	L	Z	V	K	E	F	U	F	T	X	A	A	C

Wizard · Vampire · Spaceship
Telescope · Underwater

E	J	E	V	C	B	F	R	T	G	V	X	S	K	D	J
N	S	M	O	N	K	S	N	C	E	Y	E	A	A	V	W
F	M	F	O	M	A	X	U	I	G	U	Z	G	U	M	Q
S	C	Q	V	Z	W	L	O	S	A	N	G	E	L	E
P	J	J	B	A	D	E	Y	P	W	P	I	H	I	Y
U	V	W	U	A	B	F	F	F	S	D	R	E	K	O	N
S	I	E	C	D	W	C	H	I	C	A	G	M	M	P
A	G	S	F	M	Y	Y	W	N	L	M	Z	B	R	I
K	W	X	W	S	S	B	R	W	I	R	D	J	C
T	A	L	U	C	Q	E	X	V	O	A	P	W	O	A	A
M	L	N	O	B	B	B	R	R	B	F	I	C	Q	B	W	L
A	V	F	L	A	M	J	U	H	I	P	B	X	X	M	U
D	D	G	M	D	F	V	M	J	L	S	E	B	O	I	M
Q	I	E	F	M	O	F	H	E	V	W	N	A	D	C	S
Z	T	K	P	B	I	C	L	D	X	Q	E	K	T	F	M
E	Y	B	O	O	J	Z	E	D	L	X	P	K	N	F	Y	T
Q	H	S	X	Z	V	A	O	U	F	Z	T	E	I	Q	B	K

Miami · Chicago · New York
Los Angeles · San Francisco

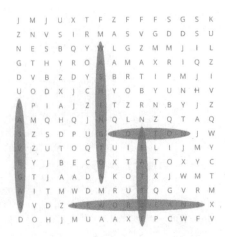

J	M	J	U	X	T	F	Z	F	F	F	S	G	S	K
Z	N	V	S	I	R	M	A	S	V	G	D	D	S	U
N	E	S	B	Q	Y	L	G	Z	M	M	J	I	L
G	T	H	Y	R	O	A	M	A	X	R	I	Q	Z
D	V	B	Z	D	Y	B	R	T	I	P	M	J	I
U	O	D	X	J	C	Y	O	B	Y	U	N	H	V
P	I	A	J	Z	I	T	Z	R	N	B	Y	J	Z
M	Q	H	Q	J	N	Q	L	N	Z	Q	T	A	Q
Z	S	D	P	U	G	D	T	O	J	W
Z	U	T	O	Q	T	U	I	E	L	I	J	M	Y
Y	J	B	E	C	O	X	T	A	T	O	X	Y	C
T	J	A	A	D	K	O	T	X	J	W	M	T
I	T	M	W	D	M	R	U	Q	G	V	R	M
V	D	Z	N	E	W	O	R	L	E	A	N	X
D	O	H	J	M	U	A	A	X	P	C	W	F	V

Boston · Seattle · Las Vegas
Washington · New Orleans

Q	Y	B	P	L	U	J	S	O	N	Y	P	C	W	F	I
N	X	F	K	O	M	S	J	O	O	H	E	Y	N	V	U
V	Q	S	J	L	W	E	P	O	G	B	J	X	I	C	Z
K	Q	L	X	V	I	D	O	L	Z	E	E	W	F	D	Y
S	Z	G	F	I	F	L	K	Q	A	I	Z	H	I	K
U	U	Z	P	J	L	G	U	N	C	S	Y	D	Q	A
E	G	I	D	P	E	D	E	N	V	U	P	L	F
Z	C	P	A	I	S	N	P	M	B	C	F	I	P	C	H
T	F	K	N	J	S	D	F	A	B	T	A	N	Q	U	K
D	H	X	D	V	Z	A	P	T	X	U	S	Z	Y	M
L	B	U	P	A	M	A	Q	N	D	X	M	Z	A
T	U	D	F	E	S	G	D	U	M	L	U	U	I	Y	W
U	Y	P	Q	K	L	L	T	U	R	A	C	A	G	J	M	Z
R	J	A	R	P	N	R	N	S	A	N	D	I	E	G	O	K
L	J	R	I	G	Y	D	R	N	V	T	X	G	X	K	S	L
K	T	F	Q	P	Y	D	F	P	C	L	Z	U	T	B	J
X	A	J	N	G	C	M	S	Y	T	F	G	A	O	O	Z	V

Denver · Orlando · Atlanta
San Diego · Philadelphia